RUTHLESS

A STEAMY, ENEMIES TO LOVERS, FLING DARK MAFIA ROMANCE

STRUCK IN LOVE ANTONIO AND SABRINA BOOK ONE

CHIQUITA DENNIE

304 PUBLISHING COMPANY

AUTHOR INSPIRATION

"Never allow anyone to steal your joy. It doesn't matter how many times someone says you can't do something. Invest in yourself—even if it's just writing down what your goals and plans are. Starting small can lead to bigger things."

—Chiquita Dennie

LATEST RELEASES FROM CHIQUITA DENNIE

Latest Releases from Chiquita Dennie

Antonio and Sabrina: Struck in Love 1, 2, 3,4

Heart of Stone, Book 1 (Emery & Jackson)

Heart of Stone Book 1.5 Emery &Jackson A Valentine's Day Short

Janice and Carlo: Captivated By His Love

Heart of Stone, Book 2 (Jordan and Damon)

Temptation

Heart of Stone, Book 3 (Angela and Brent)

Bossy Billionaire

Cocky Catcher

Joaquin Fuertes (Fuertes Cartel Book 1)

ReFuel

Pressure

Upcoming Releases (2021/2022):

Heart of Stone, Book 4 Jessica and Joseph

Joaquin Fuertes (Fuertes Cartel Book 2)

She's All I Need

Exposed - A Salvation Society Novel

DISCLAIMER

This work of fiction contains strong language and explicit sexual content and is only intended for mature readers. This story may contain unconventional situations, language, and sexual encounters that may offend some readers.I would recommend another book. This book is for mature readers (18+).

INTRODUCTION

Are you signed up for my newsletter?

Join today and find out all the latest in new releases, contests, giveaways, sneak peeks and more.

www.chiquitadennie.com

SYNOPSIS

Struck of Love never felt so good...

Twenty-four-year-old Sabrina Washington is a strong, proud African American woman, the daughter of Jonathan and Candice Washington, they were constantly the most talked about and wealthiest family in New York City. One night, Sabrina falls head over heels in love with the most dangerous man she's ever come across.

Sexy Italian Antonio De Luca has long been the object of countless women's attention as the owner of many popular nightclubs throughout New York City and his reputation as the son of the most notorious mobster in New York hasn't hurt his love life any. Ladies always love a dangerous enigma.

Will their two worlds combine, or will the dangerous lifestyle tear them apart?

CHAPTER 1

SABRINA

I had the worst possible day, and now my two best friends dedicated themselves to getting me out of my funk. I'd been dealing with a sixty-hour work week, clients running late, and my family constantly harping on my failed engagement. Tonight could be great and exactly what I needed, or it could turn out to be epically dreadful.

For the past few weeks, my ex had been trying to swindle his way back into my life.

Not today, Satan.

I refused to deal with his lies and cheating.

I pulled up to the exclusive, trendy nightclub, Ryde— they'd been open for only a year and had quickly earned a reputation for hosting high-profile actors and models throwing lavish parties. Janice had texted and said she had a table already reserved. I was glad because she knew this long stretch of people standing outside in line wouldn't work for my mood.

"I need a drink after the day I've had," I mumbled under my breath as I got out of the car and approached the door.

I attempted to go around the bouncer, and it was just my luck that he was feeling himself big time.

"Name, please?"

I perused the line behind me, turned back toward the bouncer, and narrowed my eyes at his nametag.

"Ronald," I mumbled under my breath. With a name like that, I'd be bitchy all day, too. "Really, we're playing this game?" My short fuse was about to burn down. His eyes shifted from the grumbling and raucous shouting of the crowd back to me.

"Lady, I don't care who you are, this is my job. So, again, name?"

I was desperately trying to not go off on this guy. The way I was set up, people should think twice about stepping up to me.

I relaxed my shoulders, shifted my weight from one foot to the other, and put on the best smile possible.

"Sabrina Washington."

He smiled back, slowly unhooked the velvet rope, and gestured for me to enter. I rolled my eyes at his arrogance. He'd be lucky to have someone like me mentioned at his club. The Washington name rang bells on New York Wall Street.

I walked into the club as Chance the Rapper's "No Problem" blared. The crowd was thick, and people stood wall to wall.

My head reeled from all the weed smoke wafting in my face.

"Jesus, no wonder it's the top club in the city. They let you do just about anything in here."

Finally spotting Janice and Liz, I attempted to walk over and got stopped by some guy bumping into me. "Damn, lil mama, I didn't see you there."

"It's fine."

I started to walk off, and he jerked me back into his chest. "What's the rush?" I glanced at his hand still holding onto my arm and jerked away from him.

"Look, I'm not one of these lil girls that fall all over the guy in the club, flaunting his money. You'd do well to keep your hands to yourself, buddy."

He smiled and held his arms up in a surrendering stance.

"My bad, gorgeous," he whispered in my ear. "You need some dick. Let your boy help you out."

I waved him off and walked over to my friends at the bar.

"All right, I'm here. Now let's get this over and done before I get annoyed."

Liz and Janice pulled me into a group hug.

"Aren't you looking lovely?" Liz asked.

Janice looked at me curiously.

"What?" I harshly screamed out.

"We're working on getting you out of this rut, but we need you to meet us halfway." I bit my bottom lip, looking around the room, attempting to dodge her questions.

"Listen," I took a deep breath. "I've had a long day at work and dealing with Alex's bullshit has left me more than a little annoyed."

Janice held her hand up, cutting me off.

"What you're not going to do is play the sad, depressed bitch role tonight. No, ma'am. Remind me again of how we became friends."

Both girls grabbed me by the arm, and our drinks were placed immediately in front of us. We snatched them up and walked over to our table.

Before we even sat down, Janice went in on my breakup.

According to her, he was 'the scum of the earth, who called off the engagement one week before the wedding.'

Janice Campbell was what you would call classically beautiful. Standing at five foot seven, with dark-brown skin, she had long jet-black hair that hung down to the middle of her back with an hourglass, shapely figure. She was gorgeous without having to do anything.

The attitude was the biggest difference between us. Janice would tell it like it was. She was born without a filter and didn't care whose feelings she hurt in the process. Liz was the quiet one, but she had a little fire in her if you caught her on the right day.

Liz Williams was five foot five, curvy, and had deep-brown eyes, pouty lips, with short, natural curly hair. Her life was all about living to be her best self, something out of *Fix Your Life* with Iyanla. She was a vegetarian, eco-friendly, save the planet type of chick. She'd always been the one to get me to take better care of myself and leave the stress of work behind. She would set up self-care spa days or girl trips to relax and live more fully by embracing life.

Then came me. Standing at five foot seven with a flat stomach, curvy hips, thick thighs, full lips, and chestnut-brown skin, I had a reputation for being very stubborn and hardheaded, to say the least.

"Hey, can we get another round of drinks over here? My God, look at the men in here tonight. It's like an all-you-can-eat buffet in here," Janice said, extending her hand toward the waitress.

"Yeah, I'm not feeling up to these guys. Maybe I should head home and drink my sorrows away in private," I mumbled slowly.

"Oh, no, you don't. This is exactly what you need,

alcohol and gazing upon all the sexy scenery," Liz yelled over Janice's ear at me.

"Listen, Sabrina, we know it's tough, but you've been holed up in the house for the past few weeks. It's time to get out and mingle a little," Liz said.

"We're not saying marry the next guy you meet; just get laid." Janice pointed around the room toward all the guys passing drinks around.

The girls danced in their seats to the beat of the music. Loud music blasted throughout the club, and people were dancing and grinding up on each other.

As I took a sip from my drink, I felt someone watching me. I drowned out the talking and noticed this guy staring right at me from across the room. He smiled. I freely glanced at him up and down. I felt like my heart was about to burst out of my chest. Since the moment I met Alex, no man had ever made me feel this strong pull, and I needed to slow it down because there was no way in hell I would travel down that road again.

The man was Antonio De Luca, the twenty-seven-year-old most eligible bachelor in all of New York City. Standing at six foot two, his broad shoulders, gorgeous ocean-blue eyes, firm jawline, and two dimples made my heart skip a beat when he smiled at me.

Suddenly, I felt nervous, like a teenager again with butterflies in my stomach. Not only was he the sexiest man I had ever seen, but he was surrounded by women and men hanging in his section like a celebrity. Jealousy was my name and scared was the game.

Janice noticed out of the corner of her eye what had captured my full attention. She nudged me in the arm.

"Hey, if you look any harder, you both will start a fire."

"What are you talking about?"

Hopefully, no one else noticed our moment.

"Uh-huh, if you look at that guy any longer, you're going to get pregnant."

"Who are you guys talking about?"

Liz looked toward my line of sight.

"Nothing; let's go dance. I'm here to have fun, not sit and sulk."

Janice jumped up and grabbed Liz's hand. She led the way to the dance floor as I followed. All three of us danced together in unison to the latest Beyoncé track.

A crowd formed around us as we danced in a circle.

"Get it, girl!" Janice screamed over the loud music.

"Bitch, I can't hang with you no more; my back hurts."

Janice nudged me in the side of my hip and slapped my ass. She watched as I made it clap back.

Yes, my ass bougie could dance. Looking behind me, I saw Liz grinding all up on some guy.

Janice and I walked toward them and moved our hips in sync to the beat of "Single Ladies." We pulled Liz with us, and her dancing partner pulled out some money and threw it at us. Janice's crazy ass picked it up and tucked it in her bra. The DJ turned the light strobes on, as the bass of the music drowned out all the way up high and asked for everybody to scream.

"Now throw your hands up! Let me see the ladies," the DJ yelled, extending the mic toward the crowd.

"Aren't you glad you came out tonight?" Janice asked, coming near me and grasping my hand as she twirled in the middle of the dance floor.

"It's still early, so I'll be the judge of tonight," I replied jokingly. I fanned myself, then leaned toward our table to grab a napkin to wipe the sweat beads off.

"When's the last time you've been out?" Liz asked.

"I don't know, maybe a few weeks," I answered.

"Try three months," Janice said, snapping her fingers and swaying her hips.

"Not that long, Janice," I remarked, before I picked up my glass of champagne and took a sip.

"You've been so held up with work or angry at your ex. You've turned down every invitation to hang out," Janice complained.

"She's out now, so let's not dwell on it tonight," Liz said.

"We can't all get over heartache like you, Janice, by getting under a new man," I commented. She rolled her eyes at me.

"Life is too short, babe. Live and learn. He was never good for you anyway," Janice stated for the hundredth time.

"That's my song," Liz called out, talking about the rap group Migos with their latest hit song. Liz's hands flew up in the air, and she pointed at herself. I chuckled at her new playful nature. We stayed on the floor for a while as the music mixed in from old school to new music.

CHAPTER 2

ANTONIO

*I*t was almost one a.m., and I was chilling with my friends in the VIP area of the club. I was talking, watching the women dance in front, laughing and having a good time.

I just happened to glance over and notice a beautiful woman with her friends seductively dancing. I was so caught off guard by the smile on the statuesque black beauty that I stopped speaking. She stole the breath right out of my lungs. She was so breathtaking to me.

We made eye contact as she walked back to her seat, and neither of us could look away from the sudden heat and the strong pull we felt.

She made me so uncomfortable that I had to adjust myself in my pants from the arousal slowly making an appearance in a crowded room.

Finally, I was being drawn back to the conversation by the snap of a finger from my best friend Carlo Russo.

"Hey, you okay?"

"Yeah, I'm fine. What did you say?"

I took a sip of my drink.

"I said, let's take these lovely women out to dinner and then head back to the house for a nightcap."

Both women were sitting there, smiling inanely and rubbing on my knee like it was a magic lamp that would grant them their gold-digging wishes.

A few minutes later, some guy came up behind the beauty I was watching and must have asked her to dance. She hesitated and took a step back, looking around. The music turned to a slower song, and she wrapped her arms around his neck.

I felt agitated and frustrated by the closeness of this jerk, pushing up on my woman.

"My woman," I whispered slowly.

Damn, I had no claim on her yet, but there was no denying that I felt somewhat protective of a stranger.

The guy moved in closer and placed his face in the nape of her neck. She shrugged his head away and shook her head. As the song ended, she glanced around the room and noticed me looking. Somehow, anger overwhelmed me. I was seething to kick this guy's ass for touching what belonged to me.

The DJ played faster songs, and the guy grinded up on her. My attempt to get up and handle this douchebag was halted by one of the Doubletramp twins.

"Where are you going, Tony?" she whined.

One tramp tried grabbing my hand, and she must have felt scared by the look I gave her because she dropped it just as fast.

Still eyeing the beauty, I noticed she had gone back over to her table before I could talk to her. I decided just to play it cool before my temper blew up.

Carlo passed me a drink, and I knocked it back.

Checking my phone, I received a notification from my boys, Sonny and Lenny, telling me about a new shipment coming in tonight. Having to take on more work from my family's business, on top of opening more clubs, had me annoyed and beyond exhausted.

I replied.

Antonio: Load and land at Mama's house for dinner.

Sonny: She makes the best meatloaf.

Thinking about this deal and closing our Spain liquor deal would add a lot more dollars to our pockets. Sonny replying in delight about something meant that everything was fine in code and helped to keep things off the feds' radar in case any of our people got held up. It also made me feel better about the situation.

I decided to get up and head to my office to finish some paperwork before leaving.

While noticing my black beauty standing and dancing so close to other guys and watching their hands roam all over what belonged to me, my blood boiled. I thought of stepping in and pulling her toward me.

"What the fuck am I doing?"

I shook the thoughts of her out of my mind. This would never work. After dealing with Camilla for so long and then her betrayal, my heart was cold and closed off to the idea of new relationships. The only thing on my mind was fucking and fleeing. They didn't even come to my place.

"Hey, want to dance?"

"No, sweetheart."

She looked at me with her nose turned up as if I had made the worst decision ever. She moved in closer and slowly ran her hand up and down my chest. I gently grabbed her wrist to stop her.

"If you want to keep your tiny little hands, you'll think twice about touching me again without permission."

"You'll change your mind."

"I doubt it."

Carlo walked over to us and patted me on the back.

"April, just walk away," Carlo said.

"Carlo, tell your friend I'm the best."

"I think the entire club already knows that, April, so just take a hike, and we'll send a waitress to you with free drinks."

I shook my head at her stomping off and pouting like a little kid.

"Have you hit that?" I asked.

"If I say yes, would you hold that against me?"

We both burst into laughter at his comment and walked back to our seats.

I raised my glass to our guests and made a toast.

"Thank you all for coming tonight. Our club is running beyond our expectations, and soon, the Spain deal will lead us into international waters. I couldn't have done this without my friend and brother from another mother Carlo."

"Cheers!"

Everyone raised their glass and took a shot. I smiled, looking over at the crowd inside our club. This was my true passion, running a chain of nightclubs and making a name for myself outside of the De Luca Cartel. I slapped Carlo on the shoulder gently and stood to walk toward my office.

"This is only the beginning," I murmured to Carlo.

"I know, brother," Carlo replied.

My father underestimated me in thinking I would only be his errand boy and sit on the throne to do his bidding, but I made a name for myself in business. Even though my place in the family was something I couldn't change, I would make sure that my dreams were still fulfilled by opening more chains of nightclubs.

I narrowed my eyes on April as she grasped my hand,

stopping me from walking away. Tonight was about me celebrating; if I wanted a woman, I'd pick who I wanted and not someone who constantly threw herself at me.

"Baby, I have a friend who can come over tonight with us," April insisted.

"Not tonight," I said, removing her hand.

"Antonio, you know how good we are tonight," April seductively stated as she pushed her hand under my jacket and ran it up my chest.

"If I was in the mood for you, I'd let you know. This isn't getting me interested," I replied as I lifted her hands away from me and continued down the hall.

CHAPTER 3

SABRINA

I looked around and noticed the girls had sat down and were talking with two guys in the back. Motioning to the left, my dancing companion knew I was heading back to my section.

"Thanks for the dance."

He smiled and placed a kiss on my cheek.

"Can I call you sometime?" he asked.

"I don't think so. I'm just getting out of something, and dating is the last thing on my mind right now."

The guy was still watching me and snapped his fingers for the girl in his lap to get up.

I walked back to my table.

"Are you having fun?"

Liz slurred, "Peachy."

I rolled my eyes at her comment and looked for the mystery man of the hour. His friend walked toward our table.

"Oh shit, I hope we don't get kicked out!" Janice yelled out. "Close your mouth before a fly gets inside."

I cleared my throat and turned to look up at this tall drink of water.

"Can I help you?"

I attempted to hold back my nervousness.

Janice stood up, swaying back and forth.

"Damn, you're hot."

"Thank you, beautiful," Dimitri replied.

He turned and looked back at his friend. He pointed at him.

"My boss wanted to meet you."

I looked over at the guy still sitting with his entourage, showcasing my best annoyed look at the audacity of this man to send someone over to order me. He must not know a single thing about confident black women.

"Tell your boss I'm a grown-ass woman. If he's this big man, then he can get up and walk to me like a gentleman."

"Do you know who he is?" he questioned.

"I know of him, and that doesn't matter to me," I said before I tilted my head to the left and crossed my arms over my chest.

"So, you know that he's the type to get what he wants," he stated and winked.

"And I'm the type to let you know I'm not the type to be bought," I fussed, planting my hands on my hips.

He headed back to his friends. After having my say, I turned, grabbed my purse off the table, kissed and hugged my girls goodbye, and walked out of the club. I passed my keys toward the valet as I checked my watch to see how late it was getting. When my car pulled up, I tipped him, thanked him, and slid inside, putting my key in the ignition. I then drove over to the local diner to grab some take-out. I parked in front of Sybil's, then ran inside to get a quick to-go sandwich.

"Sabrina, you grabbing your usual?" Cesar asked, wiping down the menus.

I leaned over the counter, rubbing my hands together to stay warm.

"Yes, please. Turkey burger and fries," I say, grabbing some money from my purse.

The employee back door swung open. I wasn't up to another man trying to tell me I belonged to him, so I ignored Jacobi. Don't get me wrong, he was cute with a long beard, he was cute, but his ego was through the roof.

"Is that my future wife?" Jacobi flirted and laid the dish bucket on the top of the counter.

"No, and don't start, Jacobi. I'm exhausted and not up to dealing with your shit," I said, handing twenty dollars to Cesar.

"You'll come around one day, sexy," Jacobi announced and blew me a kiss.

"Glad it's not today."

* * *

Twenty minutes later, I pulled into my apartment building and greeted the doorman.

We always passed each other, either during the day or at night. He was an older gentleman around my father's age.

"How are you, George?"

"Sabrina, it's been a few days since we've spoken."

Thinking back to the last time we talked, his wife was in the hospital, and I had sent flowers and a card to her.

"It has. We need to set our tea dates back up. Is everything good with Karen?"

I noticed a slight shift in his mood when I brought up his wife.

"She's slowly getting better. You know with cancer; it's an up-and-down situation, but we're determined to beat this."

I walked around the security desk and gave him a hug and kiss on the cheek.

I moved toward the elevator, thinking of a way to help his family. George had been around my family, and I knew all his kids and grandkids. The first chance I got, I would visit Karen and take her to lunch.

Soon as I pulled out my phone, my ex was calling me.

"Sabrina! Sabrina!" Alex rushed out.

"What do you want?" I asked and hit the button to my floor.

"Just hear me out please," Alex pleaded, and I scoffed at his audacity to think I should give him any of my time.

"You have five minutes."

The door closed, and the signal went out like I thought it would. I chuckled at him trying to beg for my forgiveness. I got off a few seconds later, and my phone rang again, I ignored the call and put the key in my door.

CHAPTER 4

ANTONIO

"**A**re you sure about this? I mean, we have two beautiful women willing and ready," Carlo whispered in my ear.

"I have other plans tonight. You have fun and call me tomorrow. We have a meeting at ten a.m."

Carlo and the two women got up to leave as my future wife grabbed her purse and strode out the door.

My bodyguard Dimitri walked back over with the gift I wanted to offer her.

I caught one more glance and couldn't help the smile that rose on my lips.

"What did she say?"

"She said that she's a grown woman, and it takes a big man to actually approach her, so when you become that, then you can attempt to talk to her," Dimitri said.

"What's her name?"

"She didn't give it. I think her friends are still here; maybe I can get it from them."

"Thanks, Dimitri. I'll handle it from here."

I went to approach her friends when I got a phone call

from Carlo. I heard ruffling in the background and women laughing as I waited for Carlo to speak.

"Hey, what did he say?"

I whistled for Dimitri and covered my hand over the phone. After that little insult, I sent her friends a little note with a gift by Dimitri. I sent them the VIP treatment on the house and left a note with them to deliver to the statuesque beauty from me that read, *"When the big man approaches, don't get scared."*

Dimitri approached both girls with the gift. They both scanned around the crowded club, hoping to see who paid for the bottles and left the attached note. No one stood out or approached.

Liz pointed to her last dancing partner and saw he had already moved on with another girl. Janice waved off Liz's suggestion and pointed at the group of guys walking out of the club with another girl.

Dimitri left no information other than that it was compliments on the house from the boss.

They both looked at each other and smiled. Finally, I left the club, got into an awaiting car, and headed home.

* * *

I ARRIVED and noticed a special gift at my door.

"Did you lose something?"

I looked her up and down.

She stood with a smirk on her face, a long, fitted, black dress on her body, and her breasts hanging out.

"It's only one night, Antonio."

Thinking about the night and the need to slide into some pussy before I exploded, I changed my mind and grabbed her hand. We both jumped back into my car.

"Take us to the hotel."

Pulling off, she reached over and rubbed up my thigh, slowly unzipping my pants.

"Get on the floor."

April grinned and got on her knees with a smile on her face.

"With pleasure, sir."

I lifted her chin, tilted her head back so she understood what I was about to say.

"This is a one-time thing. After tonight, don't speak to me."

"They all say that the first time."

I shook my head at her statement. If she only knew that while she was giving me a blowjob, my newfound beauty was the only thing on my mind. She gripped me from the base, kissed the top of my large girth, and slid her tongue up and down licking me while staring in my eyes. I gripped her shoulders, steadying her pace as she took me down her throat as I gasped.

"Fuck!" I muttered as my head hit the back of the seat.

"Mhmmm… you taste so good," April mumbled.

"No talking," I said, blocking out her words so I could picture the one woman I was intrigued by tonight. Her smooth, warm, brown skin and full lips did something to me.

"Shit!" I shouted as April jerked me off and sat back up in the seat. I pulled out my handkerchief in my right pocket and cleaned myself up.

* * *

FIFTEEN MINUTES LATER, we made it to the hotel, and I stepped out with April next to me. Walking into the hotel room, I headed directly to the bedroom and gave out directions.

"No kissing and no staying the night."

"Damn, Antonio, what a way to treat a lady."

"When I find one…"

She cut me off before I could finish and stomped into the bathroom.

Taking off my shoes, shirt, and pants, I waited for her to come out.

The door opened, and she was completely naked.

I licked my lips in appraisal. Even though she had slept with everyone in our organization, April kept herself looking good.

I pulled her to the edge of the wall, turned her back toward me, and covered her mouth with my hand to drown out her loud moans. Some women wanted to show out like I was their everything, and I'd possibly choose to see them again after a one-night stand. But April was only good for giving blowjobs; her sex and over-the-top movements cut the mood fast.

"Antonio! Yass, keep going!" April groaned, as she tried to reach behind to caress my chin. I grasped her hands and put them behind her back as I finished her off with one last stroke, pulled out of her, and went to clean up.

CHAPTER 5

SABRINA

Getting into my apartment and plopping down on the couch, I was exhausted from the day and night I had. Remembering Mr. Sexy made me smile and blush. I thought of his sexy lips and rock-hard body fucking me all night long.

"I can't believe he thought he could dictate who I could dance with," I muttered to myself as I removed my coat and shoes. I placed my food on the stove to grab a plate and lay out my fries and burger.

As I ate at the counter, I noticed the answering machine lighting up. Shit! Ten missed calls and five were from Alex. I deleted them all, not even waiting to listen to the messages. After I cleaned up my food and put the rest in the fridge, I headed to my bedroom. Lifting my robe off the back of my door, I strolled to the bathroom to brush my teeth and wash my face before I fell into bed to go to sleep.

* * *

EARLY THE NEXT MORNING, I showered and stood under the water, chuckling as I thought about the night before and the guy I turned down. It would be just like me to have to deal with another cocky guy who thought he could run my life. I finished up washing with my favorite mint body wash and grabbed the towel. Pulling my hair bonnet off, I combed my hair straight while standing in front of the mirror. Once I dabbed on a little foundation and lipstick, I pulled on my work clothes and heels to meet with Janice and Liz. We liked to get together before work to talk about the night we had. I hopped in my car and headed to our usual spot not far from my apartment. Ten minutes later, I eased in next to Liz's car, grabbed my purse, and went inside, noticing them already sitting down.

Janice was talking animatedly with her hands, and I laughed and bent down to give them a hug. The time read eight thirty a.m.

"So, besties, did you get any last night?" I gestured between the two.

"I wish, but no dice. What about you?" Janice pressed me for information as she cut into her pancakes.

I gave her my best 'bitch, please' look.

"Really, Janice, I just got out of a relationship. That's the last thing I need."

"Did you tell her yet?"

Liz refilled my cup of coffee.

"Tell me what?"

Janice pulled out a piece of paper from her purse and handed it to me.

I looked at it, then at the two of them. I was trying to figure out what game they were playing.

"What's this?"

"Open it. We've been dying to know what it says. You have a secret admirer at the club."

I need new friends.

"You're lucky I love you. Otherwise, I'd have smacked you for that fake swooning."

"You're kidding me, right?"

"Let's see what it says." Janice tried to pull the note from me, and I smacked her hand away.

"I don't have time for this. What did you guys do?"

"Tell us what you're thinking?" Liz asked.

"I'm thinking I need to find new friends," I said and blew out a breath, running a hand through my hair.

"He's cute though," Janice said, pouring more syrup on her pancakes.

"Hey, Sabrina, are you getting your usual?" Bristal asked, and I nodded. The Bistro was our go-to spot, and I got the same thing every time: scrambler with avocado, waffles, and fruit. Bristal filled Liz and Janice's glass of juice, and I asked for coffee.

My gaze was locked on the two most devious bitches I knew. Both my and Janice's phone rang before I could give them my undivided attention. It was an alert for an emergency at work. I hit ignore and gathered my things. We both worked for my family's company. I, as the VP of finance, and Janice was in accounting, working her way up to acquisitions and handling accounts.

"You both are lucky I need to get to work," I stated and sipped from the glass of water right as Bristal brought my coffee over to the table.

Liz pulled the note out of my hands and read it.

"Bristal, we have to go, but here's the money. Just give it to Liz, and I'll grab it from her later," I told her and gave her twenty to box up my food. Breakfast was my favorite meal that I could eat for dinner or lunch throughout the day.

I grabbed it from Liz's hand, got up, and walked out. Janice followed, and we left for the office.

* * *

Twenty minutes later, I arrived at work. We worked on the same floor, and Janice went toward her office. I stopped at my assistant's desk.

"Any messages for me, Lisa?"

My long-time secretary and friend held up the messages.

"Yes. The firm in California wanted to know about a joint venture they would like to propose." I took the messages from her hand and opened my office door as she followed me in. I threw my coat on my couch and purse on top of my table. I sat at my desk while I listened, checking through my emails and files for any new updates after our last meeting.

"Thanks, Lisa. Hold all my calls for the next three hours."

"Do you need me to rearrange any meetings?" Lisa asked.

"Let me get back to you," I said. Lisa nodded in answer and walked out as Janice came over and knocked on my door. I gestured at her to come inside.

"Do you need me in there with you?" Janice asked, flipping through documents.

"Yes. Can you bring in the claim forms and contracts?"

"Okay, meet you in the conference room in five minutes." She grabbed the rest of my paperwork from my desk and accompanied me next door. Before opening the door to the conference room, Spencer pulled me to the side. He was another coworker at Washington Mutual.

"Hey, did you speak with your father yet?" he questioned, keeping his hand on my arm. I looked down at it, and he removed it as Janice went ahead inside.

"No, why?" I asked.

Noticing his nervousness, I looked at my watch for the time, hoping he hurried up.

"Sabrina, you know we've been dancing around this thing."

I shifted my paperwork from my right to left arm. I looked around the office to make sure no one could hear us. I sighed in agitation.

"Spencer, I'm not sure what you think is happening here, but we aren't dating, talking, or friends with benefits, Tinder hookups, anything remotely like that. Now, I have work to do, and I suggest you get to your job as well."

"Because you refuse to see what's in front of you," Spencer argued.

"I'm not interested."

"Sabrina," Spencer muttered as he slid his hands in his pants.

"Do you need anything business related?" I asked.

"No," Spencer replied.

"Then I need to get to work," I remarked. Leaving him standing there with his mouth agape in shock, I walked into the conference room.

CHAPTER 6

ANTONIO

 sat at my desk in my office, thinking about the night before and the beauty that captured my thoughts. I couldn't stop thinking about her. I knew with my father grooming me to take on the role as head of the cartel, she wouldn't fit into this world of death and chaos. This life consisted of murder, money, long hours, and frequent unexplainable business trips. The moment I even thought of feeling something for her, my chest got tighter and my palms sweaty. She'd run, and I knew deep down, I'd never let her go. Besides, this family would never allow it.

Hearing a knock at the door, I saw my mother coming inside. Maria De Luca, the Donna of the family, and the keeper of all our secrets.

I rose out of my seat to walk over for a hug and kiss.

"Good morning, son." Mother kissed both my cheeks and sat in the chair in front of my desk.

"Good morning, Mama. How are you today?"

"I'm doing well, but I heard some distressing news yesterday, and I wanted to speak with you."

"What's the matter? Is it Dad, Bruno?"

"Nothing like that. I was talking with Gloria Bianchi, and she informed me that you canceled twice on her daughter for dinner."

My mom was the sweetest woman in the world, but when things in the family weren't flowing the way my father needed them to, he sent her to fix the problem.

Her gaze had me struggling with coming up with an excuse for missing her dinner plans.

"Mama, I understand you've planned this out since I was a little boy to marry someone from another cartel family, but I can't marry someone I don't love."

"Son, we want you to be happy, and if Bianchi's daughter doesn't make you happy, then so be it, but it's time you've moved on from Camilla."

She stood and hugged me tightly.

"I want grandbabies, and your father is ready to retire. He may not say it to you boys, but I know it."

"How about I make a deal with you? Let me find my future wife on my own, and when the time is right, you'll be the first to know when the grandbabies are coming."

Mom smiled and gently ran her hands across my cheek.

"Don't forget about Sunday dinner."

She looked around my messy office as she left.

"I won't, but I have a meeting in a few minutes. Can you see yourself out?"

"Of course, and Antonio, I love you."

Hearing that made me smile at the woman who loved me unconditionally. I decided to head over to Ryde early to handle some last-minute paperwork.

Salvatore, my driver, was outside waiting.

"Ryde or home?"

"Ryde."

"Salvatore, how long did it take you to want to get married to Angela?"

He turned toward me in shock at my question.

"Kid, are you serious?"

"Yeah."

"Something that you just know," Salvatore answered.

I never looked at myself to want to get married or even be committed to a woman but thinking back on first seeing her in my club, and the way her eyes drew me into her soul, I needed to know her and make her mine.

Growing up, Salvatore was always around. He was Dad's driver, as well as his best friend. We called him Uncle Sal whenever we wanted something we couldn't get from our parents.

"I don't know. It's just this girl I saw the other night at the club that has my mind going in circles. I'm thinking of the possibilities of settling down."

"The king of one-night stands wants to get married and have kids?" He erupted in laughter.

"Not yet. There's this woman who caught my eye," I said, shifting in my seat, thinking about her reaction to my note.

"She must be really important to you," Salvatore said, stopping at the red light.

"She will be."

"What do you think your father will say?" Salvatore asked, and my jaw twitched in anger, thinking about him never accepting who I chose to love.

"I don't know and honestly don't care."

"Then you're officially the Don," Salvatore joked.

I let out a small laugh as well. We both knew I had a reputation for being single and having women in rotation. Now seeing the woman across the room had sparked a glimpse of what marriage could be if she'd have me. The light changed, and he went right, taking the shortcut through traffic toward my business.

* * *

A HALF HOUR LATER, I arrived at the club and shook hands with the security guys outside. Walking inside, I greeted all my staff who stood around talking and preparing for tonight and walked toward the bar for a drink.

"The usual, Boss?" Marco the bartender asked.

I nodded in agreement. I looked over my shoulder and admired the layout of the building. Already, the press was talking about the opening night of the club and the celebrities who came in and hung in the VIP area. Tonight would be another all-nighter of handling paperwork and ordering more supplies for the bar. I took a shot of scotch and motioned for another. When he poured more in the glass, I tipped him fifty and checked my watch. Grabbing my drink, I went to my office. As I checked the inventory numbers, I felt my phone vibrate in my pocket. I slid it out and saw a text from April.

April: Baby, can I see you again?

She then sent a picture of her in bed, squeezing her breasts. Once I finished in the hotel, I left and never looked back. She got too comfortable thinking we would become something more.

Me: Lose my number.

April: So, you didn't have a good time?

Me: Don't flatter yourself.

I blocked her number and continued managing the club affairs for the day. I called the bartender in so we could do a walkthrough of the bar.

"Yeah, Boss," Marco said, knocking on my door.

"Do you have the list of inventory we need?" I inquired.

"I have the list at the bar. Let me grab it quick."

"Also, do you have the schedule planned out for the month?" I asked, tossing a file in the trash can.

"Based on the numbers from the opening, we might need to get two more part timers to help ease traffic," Marco stated, and I nodded in agreement.

"Okay, put a call in with the temp agency and set up interviews." Marco left to grab forms, and I continued going through emails of potential business prospects. A few minutes later, Marco came back in with two stacks of paperwork for all my clubs, and we ran numbers and set up the next drop off.

CHAPTER 7

SABRINA

I leaned in and listened as the director of equity, Jeremy Smith, talked about upcoming figures for Manor Investments. Remembering the note had me smiling and contemplating.

When the big man approaches, don't get scared.

I laughed aloud, and everyone in the room turned and looked at me.

Janice gave me a peculiar look.

"Sorry, please continue."

Two hours later, the meeting was over, and I walked back to my office. Janice ran up behind me.

"What the hell was that all about?" Janice bumped my shoulder, waiting for a response.

"Nothing."

"Does this have anything to do with that note we gave you?"

"Let's go to my office."

"Yes, please. I need all the juicy dirt."

As we walked back to my office, we saw my father approaching. "I'll meet you in my office."

I gave her my papers for her to take with her.

"Order us some lunch."

"Anything specific?" Janice asked me as my dad approached and kissed us both on the cheek.

"Anything is fine."

"Hi, Dad."

"Hi, Mr. Washington."

Janice walked away.

"Hey, sweetie."

"Hi, Sabrina. How are things going on the Manor contract?" Dad asked.

I locked my arm around my father's arm, and we walked back to my office.

"It's going well. We just left a meeting with the director of investments. Things are looking up."

Dad released his arm and grabbed my hands, looking into my eyes.

"I doubt you want to talk about that, so how about you tell me what the real problem is."

He nervously pondered his next thought.

"I got a call from Alex yesterday. He wanted to apologize to us and wanted to meet with you."

He looked into my eyes.

Feeling my blood boiling, I said, "I'm sorry he called you, but this is none of your business."

I paced back and forth in front of the desk.

"If he calls you again, tell him to kiss my ass." I needed to throw something. "How dare that son of a…"

My father pulled me into his arms and held me as if he could heal all my problems and control the burning rage simmering in my gut.

"Sabrina, the guy made a mistake. He loves you. Just give him a chance to make it right."

Don't get me wrong, I loved my father with all my

heart. I always had the utmost respect for him. Looking into his eyes and seeing the stress it caused my family to have to worry about me, made the idea of cutting Alex's balls off and feeding them to him even better.

"Let's be clear about this; my personal life has nothing to do with you. I love you and Mom very much, but this issue is closed. I have a meeting right now, and I'll call you later."

I kissed my dad goodbye and got back to work. Janice walked in with bags of food.

"Hungry?" Janice questioned, holding the bag up before setting everything down on the table.

"What was that all about?" Janice stood and went into the bathroom to wash her hands.

"Alex's trying to get back with me by going through my dad."

"Are you serious? That asshole," Janice fussed, dried her hands off, and shook her head.

"We shouldn't let him ruin our day. So, tell me what happened last night after I left," I said, coming over to sit next to her to eat.

"First, we talk about that note you received."

"It's nothing. This guy sent his bodyguard over to me like I was supposed to move at the snap of a finger, be impressed, and fall at his feet. I basically blew him off, and he sent this note." I bit into the BLT sandwich and popped a fry in my mouth. Putting the sandwich down, I grabbed the note out of my pocket.

I handed over the note to Janice so she could read it. Liz walked inside, rubbed her hands together, and snatched it out of her hands.

"I vote for him. Was it the guy I saw you staring at from across the room?" Liz implied with a wink and a nudge.

She picked up the other half of my sandwich and took a bite.

"First off, I wasn't staring. We just happened to look at each other at the same time. Secondly, this is my life; no one gets a vote. Third, I'm not going out with anyone, okay?"

She popped a grape into her mouth and gulped her drink down fast to avoid commenting. This was weird for her because she always had something to say.

"What did you do? I better not end up in some sex club."

I tossed my napkin at her.

Thinking about Mr. De Luca had me a little hot under the collar. It had been well over a few months since I had sex, and hearing the rumors about him, I'd probably end up with a broken back, a sore pussy, and walking with a limp.

"He got you thinking about him."

I scoffed at the suggestion of me thinking about a hook up with him.

"Worry about yourself, and have you, Jezebel, had any dates lately?"

"Look at her trying to change the subject."

Janice teased me by making googly eyes and kissing noises.

"Girl, you need therapy."

"That's nothing new, but you need some dick and that back broken in."

"Is that the only thing you think about?" Liz queried and kicked her feet up on the table.

"No, I also think about the head game as well," Janice said cheekily.

All three of us keeled over in laughter. I took a sip of the bottled water and wiped my mouth.

"Life is about more than sex, Janice."

"Tell that to someone who's not getting any," Janice stated and smirked.

"Well, it doesn't matter because I'm not going out with him," I said.

I was determined to keep that promise and not let Antonio De Luca get into my head.

"The club was all over the gossip blogs about the opening," Janice said, pulling up some pictures of the blogs.

"Hopefully, they don't have us on anything," I said.

"No, it was more on the club itself and the owners Antonio and Carlo," Janice mentioned, scrolling through the pictures.

"You two keep dreaming about them, but I need to finish my work," I said, as I wrapped up my sandwich and gathered everything I needed for my client while they laughed and talked.

CHAPTER 8

ANTONIO

*L*eaving the club, I went home to change. I noticed my father calling. I was tempted to not answer, but he'd continue calling until I did. I saw Salvatore a few feet up from the club, so I walked over and opened the door before he got up and opened it for me. I told him all the time I didn't need him opening my doors.

"Hello, Father."

He answered in a frustrated tone, "Hello, son, where are you?"

"I'm leaving for a business meeting. What's up?"

"Get over here to the restaurant. We need to talk," my father said.

"Father, I need to get over to Ryde. Can this wait?"

"Antonio, I won't ask you again." I groaned at his response, and he hung up on me. I threw the phone down on the seat and ran a hand through my hair.

I got into my limo and told Salvatore about the change of plans. Holding my tongue with my father would only go for so long before we came to blows.

As the driver pulled up to the restaurant, I grabbed my phone and called Carlo to push my meeting back.

"Hey, I had to stop at the restaurant. Hold off on the meeting until I get there."

"I figured when your pops called me looking for you, that you'd be late tonight. I'll hold them off as long as I can," Carlo muttered through the phone before hanging up. I ran a hand down my face, exhausted from the night before, and gestured for him to speed it up and get through the traffic.

Ten minutes later, I walked into the family restaurant that my father built and greeted all the mafia Dons at the table. I walked over to the head of the table to greet my father, Don Jimmy De Luca.

"Glad you could join us, son. Please, sit."

I sat to the left of him as he started talking.

"Gentlemen, thank you for coming. I've called you all here because we have a business matter coming up that is highly sensitive, and I want to make sure it's taken care of with no interruptions."

Glancing at my phone, I saw it vibrating, and everyone stopped watching my father and stared at me. Seeing Sonya Bianchi flash across my screen had me pissed. I shut the phone completely off and focused back on the meeting.

"We have some investments overseas coming in real soon, and I want everyone to understand this very clearly. This deal is going through, and no one will fuck this up. Are we clear?" Father spoke.

Pops glanced around the room and ended at me with a strained look on his face. I narrowed my eyes at my father for embarrassing me in front of the other Capos. His actions made me want to get up and walk out.

"I called you all here because I want everyone deserving of my loyalty to be a part of this deal, but that means you understand that it is contingent upon me getting complete participation from everyone here. I value everyone's opinion, but don't mistake my position as Don of this cartel. You will obey my orders. Do I make myself clear?"

My father scanned around the room at each person nodding in agreement and ended with me once again.

I started to speak but closed my mouth instead.

"You're dismissed, except for you, Antonio. I need to have a word with you."

Everyone left the restaurant, and the bodyguard locked the door. I started to get up to leave.

"Sit, son."

"Dad, let me…"

"Silence, I said sit. Are you disrespecting my request of sitting at the table?" he yelled.

I sat back down and placed my phone on the table.

"I spoke with your mother today, and she informed me about the Camilla and Adriana situation."

"I have no situation with Adriana or Camilla."

"The Bianchi and Ricci families run deep, and we need them in line with our family. I could care less whether you have a whore on the side or not, but this is happening. It's been planned for many years, and you will marry Camilla." I shifted in my seat and turned my chair so I could face my father as he spoke, "I understand you may not love her now, but in time, this will change."

"Was marrying my mother an arrangement?"

Dad tapped his fingers on the table to keep from hitting his youngest son. This arrangement for marriage wasn't what I wanted for my life, no matter how much he tried to intimidate me.

"Antonio, look around you, son. This is all yours, and everything I've ever done has been for my family. I won't apologize for that. I've loved your mother from the moment I saw her, and we've been together ever since. I never told you this, but I was married to someone else when we met."

"That was an arranged marriage, and we both knew it wouldn't last. You may not believe me, but I want you to be happy. I'm the Don of the family, and one day, you'll be the Don. With that comes sacrifice. I've been patient, but all the families see your lack of commitment to the family business. We've held off long enough, but it's time you come in fully."

"I understand, and I'll make you proud. Let me at least find my wife the way you found Mom. I want the thirty years of stories and fights that you guys have."

My father groaned in response. He got out of the chair and walked toward me to say goodbye.

"I'll make a deal with you, and it's non-negotiable. You fully participate in the family business, and you can still run your little club. We still need the legitimate dealings, and I'll allow this one request of marrying whomever you choose. But let me be clear, son. Your priority is this family, do we understand each other?"

I nodded in agreement.

"I agree with those terms, Don Jimmy De Luca."

Leading my dad outside, we shook hands and hugged, and he held my face in his hands. He must think he's The Godfather.

"Good, and don't forget dinner Sunday. Your mother keeps bugging me that you don't eat enough."

He smiled and left in the limo as I left in my car.

I arrived back at my club, and the clients from Spain were waiting in the conference room. I greeted each guest with a handshake as I attempted to look around for Carlo.

Carlo sprinted into the room, disheveled, and leery eyed. Carlo greeted me with a handshake. I held a tight grip on Carlo's hand, looking him straight in the eyes to see if something was wrong.

"Gentlemen, thank you for coming out today. This has been a long time coming for all parties, and I'm extremely excited to get this deal signed today."

A knock on the door interrupted me as I was speaking. Bruno De Luca came into the room with his friend Gino Giuseppe. I tried not to expose my anger at the interruption. Knowing the reason Carlo came in flustered explained everything.

I looked over at Carlo, glaring at my brother.

Bruno walked over and kissed me on the cheek. Bruno De Luca was twenty-nine years old and the spitting image of my father and mother, except his attitude was meaner, void of empathy and compassion for anyone.

I gestured for him to have a seat as I continued talking. Bruno sat with Gino, and they stayed silent as the meeting went on.

"As I was saying, we've wanted this to happen for a very long time, and we feel this will benefit both businesses very well. So, without further interruptions, let's sign on the dotted line and celebrate."

As we started signing the paperwork, someone knocked at the door. I motioned for Carlo to answer it.

He got up and opened the door.

"What are you doing here?" Carlo asked.

Knowing how my brother operated, I knew he was just as crazy as me when he was pissed off.

"Who's at the door, Carlo?"

He opened the door more so I could see our guest. Placing my pen down, I grew heated at her being in my place of business, uninvited.

"Hi," Camila said.

"What do you want, Camilla?"

I narrowed my eyes at Camilla, then glancing over to Gino and Bruno, I could feel my blood pressure going up.

Before I did something crazy or stroked out, Carlo spoke up first.

"Listen, Camilla, you need to come back another time." Carlo nudged her out the door.

Camilla screamed and banged on the door as my phone vibrated, cutting her off. She thought because my father was okay with this business deal, I should forever forget everything that had happened. Once she betrayed me, I'd never waver from completely cutting her off and sometimes getting rid of the problem. I would be a fool if I took her back and married her. She was lucky her family was valuable to my father. Otherwise, she would have been dealt with a long time ago. People wondered why my heart had hardened over the years—she was the main reason. I'd never again take her seriously. I silenced my phone and slid it in my pocket, then rubbed my temples. Today was important, and any distractions would not be tolerated.

CHAPTER 9

SABRINA

As I sat at my desk daydreaming about Mr. Sexy and his note, picking it up to read it over again, Lisa knocked on the door. I motioned for her to come inside.

"It's five thirty. Did you need anything else before I left? All the paperwork for the Manor account was completed and sent off for the last run through, and we've started on transferring over new data for you to check up for upcoming meetings this week."

"Thanks, Lisa, I'm good; you can take off. Have a good night."

"No problem. I'll see you tomorrow."

She walked out and left for the day. For the next two hours, I finished up emailing and returning calls for the upcoming week. After catching up on everything, I logged off my computer and turned off the desk light. Grabbing my purse and jacket, I left the office around 7:40 that night.

Janice called just as I was leaving, and I answered on the first ring.

"Hey, are you home yet?" she questioned, as I threw my purse in the car with my jacket and checked my mirror.

"Hey, you. What's up? I'm getting into my car now," I replied as I cranked up the engine.

"I'm just at the store picking up an outfit for tonight. Are you coming?"

"Coming to what?" I turned the lights on and backed out of my employee space. I tried hard as hell to play dumb.

"Don't act dumb, Sabrina. I'm talking about Ryde tonight. We both know that note has you intrigued about who that guy is."

Feeling flushed again at the thought of the guy who straight eye-sexed with me last night, I instantly blushed.

"Listen, unlike some of us, I know I'm not intrigued or fascinated by anyone. It was nothing but a silly note, and I'm tired. So, good night." I stopped at the entrance and looked both ways before heading in traffic.

"Don't you dare hang up on me, Sabrina Giselle Washington. I swear to God, I will hunt you down and force you to make out with every guy I find tonight."

"As nice as that is, Janice, I think my days of man hunting are over. Let's just chalk it up to me knocking back too many martinis."

"Whatever helps you sleep at night, but as I was saying, tonight we head back to find that mystery guy and get you laid, or at least felt up. Liz and I will be at your place in thirty minutes. No excuses."

Before I could say anything, she hung up. I tried calling back, but it went straight to voicemail. I finally made it home, greeted the doorman, and walked through the lobby. When the elevators doors opened, I slouched in the corner, feeling a headache coming on.

Entering my apartment, I fell flat on the couch and

kicked my shoes off, dropping everything by my side. Then, I screamed into the pillow when the thought of having Janice find me some random guy tonight filled my head.

I decided at that moment and time that holding onto the past would only force me to become a bitter old woman. And I was too cute for that.

* * *

THIRTY MINUTES LATER, I heard a knock at my door before my best friends made their way into my apartment.

"Hey, are you ready? If not, I will make you suffer through Liz's sickening stories of Travis' exploits again," Janice stated, coming inside with Liz behind her and taking a seat on the couch. Both were dressed to perfection and ready to meet their future husbands.

Liz sat on my couch, flipping through a magazine and rolling her eyes at Janice as they argued back and forth in the living room. Feeling sexy, I walked out in a skin-tight, black, mini dress the stopped just above my thighs, showing off my long legs and black high-heel pumps with the back cut out. I was showing all the curves inherited from my mom. I pulled my hair up in a long braid that sat to the side, showing my sleek, toned, muscular back. My friends captured this moment with mouths wide open. They'd never seen this Sabrina, so dolled up and glamorous. Wearing bright red lipstick tonight, there was no doubt that I was out for blood and heartbreak.

Liz began to speak.

"I'm sorry, who are you, and what have you done with Sabrina Washington?"

"My God, if I didn't like dicks so much, I would marry

44

you now. Bitch, you are fucking hot. Have you seen yourself in the mirror?"

Janice made smooching sounds.

"Please, it's nothing. You both look hot as hell. I'm trying to catch up."

"I think I just got wet from looking at you," Janice teased, as she fanned herself. I laughed at her and stood in front of the mirror to check my makeup again.

Liz and I shook our heads in embarrassment. Janice shrugged her shoulders, not bothered by our chagrin in the slightest.

"And with that, it's time for us to head out." Liz grabbed a jacket and led us outside.

I picked up my purse and did one last look before locking the door.

"Did you call a car tonight?" Janice asked.

"I figured it's easier than dealing with a cab. Besides, tonight, I'm ready to see what surprises arise."

I shocked them both with my statement.

"I knew she was an undercover freak," Janice whispered to Liz.

Feeling my phone vibrate, Janice snatched it out of my hand.

"Well, damn. Okay, boss, just answer my phone, why don't you."

"It's Alex. Watch this."

Janice excitedly answered the phone and told us both to be quiet.

"Yes?" Janice asked.

"Janice?" Alex inquired.

"Yes," Janice replied.

"Where's Sabrina, Janice? I know she's there," Alex stated.

"She's in the middle of a threesome right now. If you'd

like to leave a message, I'd be more than happy to tell her after the fifth orgasm," Janice joked, and I held my hand across my mouth, bent over in laughter.

Suddenly, I heard the dial tone from Alex hanging up, and I shook my head at her. It was her life's ambition to cause more drama. I followed them to the elevator as we twisted and swayed from side to side at the night we were about to have. The doorman watched as we came out of the elevator and smiled at us as he held the door open.

"Ladies," George said.

"Like what you see?" Janice questioned and planted a kiss on his cheek.

"Janice, you know I'm an old man. I couldn't handle you unless I was thirty years younger," George stated, holding the door for us.

"You say you can always teach an old dog new tricks." Janice grinned, pinching his cheek as he laughed.

"Can you go one day without flirting?" I questioned as the limo pulled up, and the driver got out and came around to open the door for us. Janice slid in first, and I went inside second, then Liz. I crossed my legs, put my seatbelt on, and looked at my phone as it rang with Alex's name flashing across. The driver got back inside, and he left the apartment structure to take us to our destination.

CHAPTER 10

ANTONIO

I led all the guests out of the conference room after closing a ten-million-dollar deal for the club's business tonight. I was extremely excited. Also, I was pissed off that my brother interrupted things.

"What are you doing here?" I asked.

"My little fucking brother, I'm proud of you tonight. Let's go celebrate."

"Can you guys give me a minute with my brother?"

Carlo and Gino looked at each other, and then at us, as if both could tell something bad was bound to happen. They stepped out before all hell broke loose.

I wiped my hand across my face, trying to calm my temper before he spoke.

"This is my place of business, which, as I recall, you wanted nothing to do with. So, I ask you again, what are you doing here, Bruno?"

"I came here because I talked with Father, and he informed me that you'd be handling more of the family business. Since I'm heading out to Texas for two days for business, I wanted to make sure you understood what this all entailed."

"Just fucking spit it out, Bruno. We both know that you hate the thought that Dad is making me the head of the family over you."

"The truth is that I never expected my little brother to call the shots. Our father always gave you more than me growing up. In his eyes, you couldn't do any wrong. Many times, I wanted this life, and you wanted out, but he forced you into it. I willingly wanted this life. I'm noticing these days, it's much more rewarding being the enforcer and having everyone move out of your way when you walk down the street."

"I don't have time for this. Whatever you need to say, we can save for Sunday dinner if you're coming. Mom insists that you come."

"I'll be there. How about we go celebrate this little liquor deal you just made?"

Bruno held a small grin on his face as he slid his arm around my neck in a playful chokehold.

"Yeah, let's go celebrate, and don't bring up Camilla on Sunday, either. I'm tired of my love life being a main topic of discussion at Sunday dinner," I spat, pushing him away.

The club was loud, crowded, and thumping with people dancing and drinking. Then we headed over to the bar near Carlo and Gino and started drinking. Taking another shot, trying to get Camilla off my mind was a hard pill to swallow. At one point, we were inseparable, and nothing could break us apart. She thought because my father was turning the cartel over to me, she could just swoop in, and our families would support our union. Even the slightest thought of me marrying that bitch made my skin crawl. Camilla was only good for one thing, and she could barely do that right.

I looked over at the front entrance and saw my future woman walking inside, dressed as a goddess. Sabrina literally took my breath, and before the night was over, she would be mine. I tapped Marco to pass me a shot. I licked my lips, watching as she whispered in her friend's ear. Security looked over at me because I told them that whenever they came back here to give them whatever they wanted on the house.

"Damn." Marco whistled, and I turned to see what he was whistling at.

"That one with the long ponytail is off limits," I said.

"Claiming early, Boss," Marco joked, and I narrowed my eyes at him.

He raised his hands up in surrender

"You like your life, right?" I asked and took another shot.

The jealous and possessive bones in my body were itching to come out and tell every guy in here to keep their eyes off her because she belonged to me. She didn't know that, before the night was over, her future would be set. The way her curves were defined in that dress cried for me to rip it off and taste every sweet spot she'd allow my tongue to trace.

"I think you got it bad," Dimitri came beside me and said.

"I want to get eyes on her starting today," I said.

"Is that your bruised ego, or you really want to ask her out?" he questioned.

"Both." I sighed and ran a hand down my face as I narrowed my eyes at the guys trying to talk to her in my presence.

"A little bit of advice, Boss."

"Yeah."

"She's tough, so be prepared." Dimitri spoke, and I took another shot from the bar and prepared to meet my future.

CHAPTER 11

SABRINA & ANTONIO

Sabrina

Liz and Janice were drinking and gossiping while I was up dancing in front of our table. The bartender brought over drinks and some water without us even asking for anything. I was hesitant to take them, but Janice ignored me and took the first shot and asked for another round. Suddenly, Janice saw four guys standing by the bar goofing around. Janice nudged Liz, and she gestured toward the group at the bar. "What are you guys looking at that's so important?" I asked, ignoring the guy who wanted me to dance.

I turned around and immediately locked eyes with him. His presence had me wanting to take a shot just to calm my nerves. I rebuked the devil for enticing me to lust after this man.

"Girl, every guy over there is fine," Janice said.

"You think every guy is cute." Liz chortled and directed her gaze where Janice was looking.

"All of them will probably leave you with a broken

heart, so it's best to ignore them," I said as a pair of hands wrapped around my waist. I found I was behind the sexy guy I remembered dancing with the other night.

"You get sexier every time I see you," he said.

"Thanks, you're not bad looking either."

He chuckled and caressed my cheek.

"Ummmm… Sabrina."

"What, Janice?" I asked.

"You might not want to be so close to your new friend," Janice explained.

"Why?"

"Your little boo over there is watching you hard," Janice said, pointing toward the bar.

"Stop pointing that out; it's impolite," I said.

"Honey, being impolite is not the problem when it comes to the way he's glaring at that man standing next to you," Janice replied and laughed.

"I'm single, I can dance with anyone, and no one controls my movements."

I said it confidently, but the look in his eyes told me a different story. Maybe I should listen to Janice and not dance up close to anyone else for the rest of the night, but a part of me liked to do things on my own terms.

"He does seem to be intense," Liz remarked and waved at the group of gentlemen.

I cleared my throat.

"Liz, whose side are you on anyway?" I questioned and threw the napkin off the table at her.

"Keep me out of your love triangle," Liz stated, sat back, and stretched her arm behind the chair.

"I know the one next to Antonio is Carlo, but who is the third guy?" Liz asked.

I shrugged, not knowing or caring who they were if it meant more drama in my life. I was past cheating.

* * *

ANTONIO

I had a strong yearning to pull Sabrina into a kiss and mark her as mine, but I felt a jealous need to cover her up so no one else saw how beautiful she looked. She was the sexiest woman I'd ever seen, and she was looking right at me with the same need to claim as well.

Bruno noticed how I stopped talking and turned away. He looked up to see what caused my distraction. A woman wearing a little black dress, showcasing her long legs, plump breasts, and thick thighs. She was someone he knew his father wouldn't approve of bringing into the family.

He decided to have a little fun with his brother and see how far he could push him.

Bruno hit Carlo and Gino on the arm to follow his gaze as he walked over to Sabrina standing across the room.

"Excuse me, gentlemen, I see one exquisitely desirable woman that I have to talk with and get into those panties," Bruno said, walking over to the lady sitting at the table.

Bruno winked at me as he stepped toward the woman I couldn't stop staring at. She cut her eyes away and turned back around with her back to me. Both of her friends noticed Bruno approaching.

With my anger rising, Bruno approached her, placed his palm on my woman's back, and whispered in her ear. The girls must have liked what he said because of the loud laughter.

I took a shot and clenched my fists.

Carlo and Gino noticed the change in my demeanor, and they both tried to stop me.

"Get your fucking hands off me!" I shouted, in aggravation.

"Tony, calm down. We have a crowded club tonight,

and you know he's just fucking with you. Come on, just think first. Besides, who cares if he gets into this chick's pants?"

"Don't you ever talk about her again, do you hear me? She's none of your concern."

She noticed me approaching. Her eyebrows rose, and a small smile crept across her face.

Bruno moved his palm in small circles on her lower back. She quickly moved out of Bruno's grasp.

"Ladies, allow me to introduce my little brother, Antonio De Luca. He owns this club, along with many others around New York and Miami. Antonio, this is the lovely, foxy Janice, sweet Liz, and the sexy Sabrina Washington. Did I get that right?" Bruno held onto my woman's hand as he introduced everyone.

"Hello, Antonio. I remember you from the other night; you gave us the VIP treatment. I wanted to thank you for that," Janice stated.

The one introduced as Janice extended her hand and gave me a handshake. At the same time, I continued to stare at Sabrina.

"It's my pleasure to meet you, Janice, Liz, and I've never agreed on anything with my brother before, but at this moment, I have to agree. You are definitely breathtakingly beautiful and sexy, Sabrina Washington," I said as I lifted her palm to place a kiss on the back.

Sabrina tried to pull her hand out of my tight grasp, but I held on tighter, refusing to let go.

"Thank you, Mr. De Luca, but I believe you probably say that to all the women you come across," Sabrina answered.

I stepped in closer, invading her space.

"I guess you'll have to allow me to prove it to you,

because from where I'm standing, you're the only woman who's erased all past and future women I may meet."

Her so-called best friends sat quietly, watching the eye sex happening right in front of them.

"Now that we've made a brief introduction, let's get a round of drinks for you gorgeous gals," Bruno offered.

My brother walked toward the bar.

"Actually, Bruno, I need to speak to you about some business. Will you excuse us, sexy? It was nice meeting you all, and please stay and have a drink. Have fun. Whatever you need, let my people know I said it's on the house. Sabrina, I hope we'll see each other again before the night ends," I said, placing a kiss on her right hand.

"She'll be right here. Thanks, Antonio!" Janice yelled across the room.

"I can't believe you just said that. My sex life is that important to you that you have to embarrass me?" Sabrina huffed.

"You're lucky I didn't write your phone number on the bathroom wall," Janice responded, annoyed.

"Kiss my ass," Sabrina snapped, then flipped Janice off. I chortled while they went back and forth.

I waved over our waitress.

"Shit, that's the problem right now. You need somebody to kiss it, or at least lick it." Janice slapped hands with Liz.

"Bitch, I'm not gay, just overdue for some dick," Sabrina announced lowly. I looked over my shoulder, making sure no one heard us talking.

Carlo came over to the table.

"Hello, Bella. I'm Carlo, Antonio's business partner and friend. He asked me to make sure you guys are taken care of. Can I escort you to the VIP area?"

"We're fine here. You don't have to fuss," she attempted to state, but Carlo put his hands up to cut her off.

"Please, Bella. He'll kill me if I don't follow orders. I promise, we won't bite unless you ask real nicely," Carlo insisted.

Carlo looked over at Janice, smiled, and led the ladies to the VIP private area.

* * *

ANTONIO

I sat in my office, trying to calm my nerves, before Bruno appeared.

"What the fuck was that?" I yelled out.

"I was hoping for a thank you, not a fuck you."

"Fuck you, and I don't need help with a woman. Just leave and let me decide on what I need."

"She has you so speechless; it's pretty funny, slightly pathetic, but funny. What are you afraid of, Antonio?"

"How can you even ask that? I'm not exactly the typical guy she would date, or that I'd bring home to Mom and Dad if you haven't noticed… why the hell am I having this conversation with you? Get out."

"All I'm saying is that she's beautiful; what's the harm in just getting laid? You've been uptight for the longest time since Camilla left, and we both know how that situation ended. So, put us all out of our misery and just go pay for a hooker, or nail the black chick outside. I couldn't give a shit but be ready to handle the business when I get back."

I got up out of my chair. "She feels different. I can't just rush it. Besides, I don't want to just have a one-time thing or hide her from Dad. Shit, what am I saying? We haven't even gone out on a date. This is the first time I've actually spoken to her."

"Look, you're a good kid; you'll figure it out. Just don't

wait too long because from what I'm seeing, every guy in here is staring at her on the dance floor, and that ass looks extremely plump," Bruno joked.

I hit Bruno in the arm as he walked down the hall and out to the club. Bruno kissed the girls goodbye as I headed to the bar and took another shot while gazing at Sabrina dancing with her girls.

Carlo came up from behind the bar.

"Hey, what happened with Bruno?"

"My brother's an asshole," I blurted out sarcastically.

"So, what else is new?" Carlo asked. "Just go, stop thinking too much about the consequences."

I took one more shot and walked over to the table. I placed my hand on her lower back and immediately, she stood still.

"Ladies, would you mind if I steal Sabrina for a moment? I promise I'll bring her right back," I asked.

"It's up to Sabrina whether she wants to talk with you alone. She's a big girl," Liz answered.

Liz winked at me and pulled Janice away.

"That she is," I replied.

I watched her plump, rounded ass sway left and right. I had thoughts of licking and smacking each cheek as she lay flat on her stomach, trying to catch her breath from our fourth round of sex.

"I'll be right back, guys. Hold my spot."

The unbidden erection in my pants had me adjusting myself and praying no one noticed. Her lingering perfume had me on a high that I never wanted to come down from. This was my woman, and no matter who tried to come between us, they wouldn't win. I could already tell I would move heaven and earth for her.

I walked up, capturing her arm and interlocking our

hands. She stared into my eyes, then down at our hands. Her gaze instilled my desire to keep her protected. If I pursued anything serious with her, I'd have to keep my temper in check; the wrong move, and I'd kill an entire bloodline of a family.

CHAPTER 12

ANTONIO & SABRINA

Sabrina

As we headed down to his office, two women came out of the bathroom and saw Antonio. I remembered both women from the last time. They were at the club, sitting with him and his friends, looking very comfortable.

"Hey, Antonio, when are we heading back to your place? We had fun the other night," the woman asked as she ran a hand up his arm. I tried to pull out of his hold to give them some privacy, and he tightened his grip.

"I can give you two some privacy," I informed him.

"That would be great," she replied, biting her bottom lip, while a look of lust gleamed in her eye.

I stepped back and turned to go back to my table.

* * *

ANTONIO

Sabrina stepped out of my arms and began walking back to her friends.

"Ladies, please excuse me. I'll have Carlo take care of you guys. Just give me a few minutes."

"Don't let me interrupt your plans with them. It's getting late anyway," Sabrina suggested.

I was extremely pissed that she was turning away from me and leaving. I grabbed her arm tighter, refusing to let her go, and called for Carlo.

"Can you take them out and make sure no one comes this way for the next hour?"

Sabrina looked at me with annoyance and rolled her eyes.

"I'm not interested in anything you have to say. Please let my arm go."

"Let's just talk in my office. We can even leave the door open. I promise to be a gentleman," I stated.

I held my hands up in a surrendering stance. Sabrina looked into my eyes and caved to my demand. She was a headstrong woman, but after a little taming, she would be submissive to me and know that I only wanted the best for her.

I was a stranger who she felt an overwhelming need to please.

"Fine, but only a few minutes, not an hour, and the door stays open."

"Are you always this stubborn?" I questioned as I lifted her chin and peered into her eyes.

"It takes one to know one."

I led her over to sit on the couch. I poured us both a glass of wine and sat next to her.

"So, Sabrina Washington, what brings you to my club two days in a row?"

Already, I could sense she would be a challenge.

"Is that what you really want to know?"

"I'm just getting started. Trying to pace myself."

"Someone is feeling confident about himself. You think this is going somewhere?"

"I know it will."

Slowly, I moved in closer to her on the couch, putting our glasses down on the table.

"What are you thinking about?"

Slowly, she tried putting distance between us.

"I'm thinking how can you be real and be in my office right now? I feel like I'm dreaming, and someone will wake me up soon. If that happens, I'll be extremely upset that I never had a chance to kiss you. May I kiss you, Sabrina?"

She paused for a moment, thinking over my request.

Before she could answer, I raised my hand and gently caressed her cheek. Then, I placed a soft kiss right at the corner of her lips. I noticed her surprised expression.

A knock at the open door interrupted us.

"I'm busy," I called out, not wanting to let our moment be interrupted. I peered over at Carlo, avoided his smirk.

Carlo knocked again, and I groaned annoyed at his presence.

"I can't explain it, but I want to see you again. Please, let me take you out to dinner."

"I don't think that's a good idea."

Suddenly, I felt vulnerable around this woman.

"Why?" I asked.

Carlo stepped into my office.

"Sabrina's friends are ready to go," Carlo said. I was pissed at the disturbance by her friends.

"Fuck, do you have to go?" I was getting agitated with all the interruptions.

"It's getting late, and I have an early meeting tomorrow. Besides, I wouldn't want to cramp the De Luca playboy lifestyle," Sabrina murmured silently to herself.

"It's Antonio, and it's happening. Just dinner, what's the harm in that?"

"Fine, Antonio, but before this dinner, I will let you know that I'm not looking for any type of relationship. Do we understand each other?"

"We'll see about that."

I walked her out of the office with my hand on her lower back.

"How are you getting home?" I inquired.

I moved in closer, inhaling her perfume. She shifted from one foot to the other nervously.

"I have a car waiting."

Before she turned, I grabbed and kissed her hand again. She moved away from me.

"What's your angle, Mr. De Luca?"

I was going to love breaking down her walls.

"Looking to get to know you a little bit better, Bella."

We both lingered, looking into each other's eyes, trying to see if this was real.

I escorted all the women out and held her hand tightly. I opened the passenger door to let Janice and Liz in first. Then, I held Sabrina by the waist and stopped her from getting into the car.

"Dinner tomorrow, where's your phone?" I demanded, then watched as she pulled out her phone.

I grabbed it and dialed my number to save her own on my phone.

"Good night, ladies, and sweet dreams, Sabrina."

She leaned into me and whispered in my ear, "Buona Notte, Antonio."

I was stunned that she spoke Italian. I refused to let her go; she was mine. Standing there and watching the car drive off made me rethink about taking over the cartel. All my life I had been trained by my father to lead the family and become the Don after he retired. I knew bringing her in wouldn't be easy. The only way to convince my dad was through my mom; she would know what to do. No matter what, Sabrina was my future wife and the next Donna to stand beside me.

CHAPTER 13

SABRINA

"**W**hat the fuck just happened?" Janice screamed in the limo.

As Liz started to talk, I zoned out and glanced back at the man known as Antonio De Luca.

"Yeah, Sabrina, I think you have a new guy that puts Alex to shame, honey." Liz clapped and cheered me on.

"You guys, it's nothing. He just wants to take me out to dinner. Nothing's going to happen." I tried telling myself that as well, hoping I was right.

They both looked up at me, knowing it was all a lie.

"Are you trying to convince yourself of that, or us? Because from what I saw tonight... He's planning on getting into those black lace panties. But you should know before this dinner, or before anything goes any further exactly what expectations you have for yourself."

"First question, how do you know the color of my panties?

"Girl, bye. I'm constantly going through your closet."

"I knew it."

"Anyway, get back to the subject at hand, before I tell Liz about Charlie Big Dick."

My mouth flew open in shock. How did this heffer know about my vibrator? Knowing that she had the exact same one.

"My expectations are dinner and then go on with my life. Listen, Antonio De Luca will be an afterthought. I can promise you that."

"He doesn't look like the type to just want dinner," Liz stated.

As Janice spoke, my mind zoned down to my vibrating phone.

A text message from Antonio came through.

I texted back.

Antonio: Sweet dreams.

Sabrina: I guess that Big Man finally showed up. Good night, Antonio.

The driver finally dropped me off, and I went to my place.

Antonio De Luca was beyond gorgeous, stubborn, sexy, and aggressive. He took what he wanted, and I couldn't help but feel like I wasn't experienced enough to handle him.

Heading to the shower, I wrapped my hair up in a tight bun with a scarf to keep the water from ruining anything. Turning on the shower, I stepped inside, and the water was warm on my body. I leaned over, picked up the sponge, and cleaned myself. Somehow, he popped into my head again, and I slowly placed an index finger in my pussy to curb the lingering heat between my thighs.

"Ahhhh… shiiiit!"

I kept hearing his voice in my head.

"Baby, you like this?"

"Ohhh, God!!" I cried out.

"Can I have you, Sabrina?"

"Yes!"

I popped my eyes open and looked around the bathroom, trying to calm my breathing. I chuckled to myself and walked out of the bathroom with a towel to dry off. I lifted the lotion off my nightstand and rubbed it against my skin. Placing the lotion back, I grabbed my vibrator from the drawer.

"It's going to be a long night."

I lay up against the headboard, pushed the covers back, dimmed the lights, and positioned the vibrator at my entrance on low speed, while I anticipated Antonio's real touch. I couldn't believe I was even thinking of him as I pleased myself. Comparing Alex to Antonio was ridiculous; I was with Alex for years and never felt this sexual pull. Antonio was mysterious, sexy, a little demanding, someone who knew what he wanted, and let himself be the first and last thing I thought about if a relationship were to get far. I pulled the cover tighter, hearing Antonio's words in my mind about not touching myself. My orgasm was his job, and no one, including myself, should take that job away from him. I couldn't let myself fall deep into an undying love that knocked me off my path to loving another man trying to control my world.

CHAPTER 14

SABRINA

*T*wo *days later.*

I was at the mall with Janice and Liz shopping for a few things for my apartment and some new clothes. We went inside Nordstrom carrying bags we already filled with new bathing suits. I scanned the different evening dresses and held a red dress up under my chin.

"What do you think of this one?" I asked, posing in front of the mirror.

"It's cute, but too long and doesn't show enough of your shape," Janice said, picking a short black cocktail dress.

"That would be good with some silver high heels," I replied and took the dress out of her hands.

"Oohhh, okay, this one is screaming my name," Janice mentioned and twirled around with a short gold shimmery skirt.

"If you get that, I'll take this blue, off-the-shoulder dress, and we can kind of match," Liz said, standing next to Janice.

"Don't let me forget to pick up some more business suits."

"Noted. I wanted to ask, has Spencer talked to you again?" Janice asked as we wandered over to the shoe aisle.

"Besides the day at work no, and I wouldn't put it past him to approach me again," I said.

"You have all the men falling at your feet, girl," Liz spoke, passing the dresses to the employee so she could try them on.

"Yeah, men I don't want or need," I sassed as I high-fived Janice.

"Well except Antonio though. He could probably call you right now, and you'd drop everything for him," Janice told me, and I stuck my tongue out at her.

"No, because I know he's only interested in sex, and I don't need that type of situation in my life to complicate things."

"You need to relax a little more, Sabrina," Janice said as she grabbed two pairs of shoes and headed to the counter to pay. I decided on the blue and black dress, plus a few white blouses for work, and checked out. Liz came out of the dressing room wearing a cream sweater dress and stood in front of us for our opinion.

"Definitely get that one," I said.

"I knew you had a butt somewhere in there," Janice joked and slapped her on the ass.

"Where are we off to now?" Liz asked.

"I just want to grab some lunch and go home to take a nap," I responded, and they agreed. The entire week was long, and I needed a break. As we walked out of the store and stepped on the escalator to leave the mall, I had a funny feeling someone was watching me.

"What's wrong with you?" Janice asked as I looked

around the mall, checking to see if I was going crazy or not.

"Nothing. I just thought someone was watching me."

"Well, if they are, let them continue to look. If I need to pull my little pink baby out, we'll be good," Janice said, and I chuckled. She was always the fighter of the bunch and somehow became the protector. After a while, we let her have the role because arguing back and forth would end up in circles. We finally reached the parking lot, packed up my car, and drove to Sybil's for lunch.

"You know what you're having?" Janice questioned.

"Probably the meatloaf dinner since it's something I can take home for later." The restaurant wasn't too crowded, so we sat near the corner, and the waitress passed us a menu.

"Hi, ladies. I'm Cori, your waitress."

"Hi," all three of us said.

"What can I get you to drink?" Cori asked, taking our orders.

"I'll have water," I replied, since I was driving. I had a bottle of wine at home I could drink.

"Water for us as well," Liz said.

"Sure, coming right up. Are you ready to order?" Cori questioned.

"Can I get the meatloaf and mashed potatoes?" I replied as I passed her my menu. I put the straw inside the glass and took a sip while I stared out the window. It was a busy day with cars and bike riders all clogging up the street.

"I would like salad and salmon please," Liz said, lifting her menu for Cori.

"I guess I can get the spaghetti and salad," Janice told Cori who thanked us and went to put in our orders.

"How much you want to bet Antonio's making it his mission to get you to go to dinner," Janice remarked.

"He can try," I responded nonchalantly.

Liz burst into laughter.

"Not one part of you hasn't thought about him?" Liz asked.

I shrugged, not wanting to give away the dreams I'd been having of him lately.

"Between Alex and Spencer, all it's doing is bringing on another headache from a man, which is not a priority for me."

Cori came back out with a bread basket and a cup of lemons for our water.

"Your food will be ready shortly," Cori announced, and we thanked her.

"I have to confess, his brother was cute though," Liz blurted out.

"He's not your type, Liz," I said.

"A girl can fantasize," Liz said.

While we continued chatting about our busy lives at the office and our families, Cori came back out with our meals, setting the tray down, along with a slice of cake.

"What's that?" I asked.

"A secret admirer," Cori whispered and shifted her eyes to the counter. I glanced behind at crazy-ass Jacobi smirking at me.

"Another man. Damn, Sabrina, tell us your secrets," Janice whined, clasping her hands together in prayer.

"Cori, take this back and tell him no thank you," I replied before I picked up my fork.

"So, we're not going to talk about the free cake?" Liz blurted out, and we all laughed at her statement. Cori smiled, took the cake back, and walked over to Jacobi. He chuckled and threw his hands up. Lunch lasted for another two hours while we talked. Then I drove them home and fell on the couch to take a nap for the rest of the day.

CHAPTER 15

ANTONIO

I awakened in my bedroom early the next morning from a nightmare that left me drenched in sweat. I shook off thoughts of my father demanding I take more responsibility in the family business and further complicating my business dealings with Carlo.

Checking for any messages on my phone, I saw nothing demanding my attention. I jumped up and stretched, picked out a suit for the day, and laid it on top of my bed. I opened my drawer, grabbed a pair of boxers, and went to the bathroom to turn on the shower. Standing under the water, I brushed my teeth, then washed my face. Squirting bodywash in a towel, I cleaned up and stayed under the hot, scalding water, easing the tension in my muscles.

Thirty minutes later, I was finally dressed for the day, when my phone rang. I stared down at the screen, willing it to stop. I checked my tie in the mirror and placed my wallet and keys in my pocket.

"Yeah, Pops," I answered with an exasperated tone.

I knew he felt the undercurrent of annoyance in my voice.

"Someone doesn't sound like they're happy to hear from their father."

"Excuse me. Good morning, Don De Luca."

I tried to rein in my contempt for my father.

"I give you more leeway than any other man in the organization. Not just because you are my son, but your mother would never forgive me. Don't test my patience or disrespect me. Are we clear?"

"Yes. Did you need something? Is Mother okay?"

"She's fine. I need you in the office today. We have a morning business meeting at ten a.m."

"I have to go over the books with Carlo today. The deal with Spain just closed yesterday. We need to get over to Washington Finance before noon."

"I'll give you this call once. Some men don't get that. It's expected that you will be in the office every day by ten a.m. I don't care what else is going on. The family is number one priority. Did you forget our conversation?"

My father then hung up the phone without any further preamble.

"Arrgghhhh!" I screamed in anger and threw my phone on the bed.

Ten minutes later, I finally calmed myself down and sent a text to Carlo about having to miss the meeting.

Antonio: I need you to reschedule the meeting for later this afternoon around 2 p.m. I have a meeting with my father this morning.

Carlo: Did you need me with you?

Antonio: Shouldn't take long. Call and reserve a table for two at Antonio's tonight.

Carlo: Would this have anything to do with the black beauty last night?

Antonio: Just get the reservation.

Carlo: You need to rethink having dinner with her; it could get complicated. What do you think the family will say?

Antonio: I couldn't give a shit what the family thinks. Besides, it's just dinner. You sound like one of them now. What happened to Mr. Pussy Has No Face?

I could picture Carlo falling over in a fit of laughter as he read the text messages.

Carlo: I still stand by that statement, but this girl seems to mean more to you than any girl I've seen you with. I'm just looking out for my friend and brother.

Antonio: I appreciate the concern, but I can handle it.

I closed out my phone, turned the light off in my bedroom, and walked down to the kitchen to pour a cup of coffee with no cream or sugar. I checked my watch one last time before putting the cup back in the sink and walked out of the house to deal with another last-minute issue my father had dumped on me.

CHAPTER 16

SABRINA

While finishing up in my office, reading through emails and returning phone calls, Lisa walked inside.

I waved her in to have a seat.

"Thank you again, Charles. We'll be in touch, and let's set up a lunch meeting sometime next week. I'll have Lisa give you a call. Of course, she's sitting right in front of me, and she says hello." Lisa gave me a scowling look from her embarrassed face. "Talk soon, bye."

"I can't believe you just did that."

"I'm not the only one running around with nothing to do after work at night. You need to get back out in the dating game."

"My divorce was just finalized three months ago. It's too early for dating."

"I understand about breakups. Believe me, I do, but based on the advice I received from some reliable sources, which you are familiar with, I hear that it's not rocket science just to get laid."

Lisa looked off, clearly ashamed about her current lack of a dating life.

"I came in here for a reason. We have a few items we need to go over before the business trip next week," Lisa informed me.

"Sure, let's start with that because I have a very busy day, and I need everything done before my dad gets into the office today and complains about the deal."

As we talked about everything, my phone vibrated with a text message.

Antonio: Dinner, 8 pm, I'll pick you up.

Sabrina: Actually, I will meet you at the restaurant.

Antonio: A real gentleman picks up his date.

Sabrina: Seeing as we met in a club and you had multiple women surrounding you, and this is our first meeting outside the club, I'd prefer a getaway plan, just in case you leave me stranded for any new dates.

Antonio: I can meet you at the restaurant if you wish, but me leaving with another woman tonight won't be happening unless you know another Sabrina.

Sabrina: Quick question, will I need a bodyguard escort?

Antonio: Are you saying you need protection from me?

Sabrina: I'm not sure, Mr. De Luca. You tell me.

Antonio: I told you to call me Antonio. I assure you, Bella. You won't need protection from me unless you're wearing what you had on last night, and then I can't promise anything.

Sabrina: Noted, I can't make any promises. I have to confess... I liked the look in your eyes when you saw me.

Antonio: I liked the look in your eyes as well. I have a meeting I'm going into now, so we'll talk more later.

Sabrina: Yes, Mr. De Luca.

Closing my phone, I thought about last night and the many orgasms I had with my little electronic friend.

Going through my schedule for the next few weeks,

Lisa and I finished up quickly and decided to get an early lunch.

Gathering my purse, I walked out toward her desk, and we talked about any upcoming dates she had planned before we got into my dating life.

"It'll all work out, have faith."

I noticed a tear falling down her cheek.

"I'll try," she mumbled sadly.

Walking off the elevator, we linked arms and headed over to our usual lunch spot down the street. As we approached the corner stoplight, I glanced over at the car beside us and did a double take. Dumbass Alex turned toward us. The walk sign changed, and I rushed Lisa before he could catch up with us.

CHAPTER 17

CARLO

*C*arlo: *It's all set for tonight.*

    Antonio: See you at Washington Finance in an hour.

I gathered up the books and made some last-minute phone calls to reschedule the meeting. After finishing and picking up my paperwork, someone came inside.

Antonio's ex-girlfriend Camilla Ricci took a seat in front of his desk.

"How are you doing?" Camilla asked.

"Camilla, what are you doing here?"

Camilla pulled out her makeup and checked her lipstick.

"I wanted to talk with Antonio, if he's not too busy."

"He's not here, and that's a bad idea."

She placed her compact back in her bag.

"Carlo, please, it's time to move on and forget the past."

Camilla waved me off.

She got up and walked toward me. She slightly patted my chest and fixed my tie.

"Just tell him I stopped in. I'll be back."

"Camilla, don't do this. It'll mess with his head. Antonio has finally moved on from you."

"Well, maybe it's time he remembers why we worked so well together. Is Bruno around?"

"No, and that wouldn't help the situation."

"I promise, Carlo, I just want to talk. What does he need protection from little old me for?"

Camilla winked and walked out with a mischievous look that I knew all too well.

She was planning something, and knowing the Ricci family, Antonio was the target. I couldn't let that happen.

My phone vibrated with a text message from Bruno.

Bruno: Meet me at the warehouse.

* * *

I HOPE you enjoyed Antonio and Sabrina's story so far. Continue with "*Savage Book 2* https://books2read.com/u/bpED6g and then "**Beast Book 3** of Antonio and Sabrina here https://books2read.com/u/3LpgdJ . If you love billionaire romance check out "**Heart of Stone 1**" **here** https://books2read.com/u/boWPAV with a host of characters intertwined.

Check out Mafia romance here "*Antonio and Sabrina Book 1*"https://books2read.com/u/4AxKLo

Please also check out my **Mutual Agreement** " https://books2read.com/u/mgzzWX a steamy political romance.

Have you checked out "**She's All I Need**" click here https://books2read.com/u/49lkeW a sports, opposites attract romance.

"**Heart of Stone Book 4**" **here** https://books2read.com/u/4NXyPG with a host of characters intertwined.

Follow Desiree and Gabriel in "*Temptation?*" It's a standalone contemporary, sports, curvy girl romance.

Check it out here https://books2read.com/u/mle1Vv Check out **Aydin a grumpy boss, bodyguard romance** here https://books2read.com/u/mBwaOy .Follow my standalone opposites attract, age gap, military romance "**Exposed**" https://books2read.com/u/bQyYZe . Are you a fan of sports romance? Then download one-night stand, billionaire romance "**Refuel**" https://books2read.com/u/boDyDA. Also, follow it up with workplace, sports romance "**Pressure**" https://books2read.com/u/3Ly1r7 .If you love romantic comedy, fake relationships, enemies to lovers, find it here, "**Something Gained.**" Click the link https://books2read.com/u/baGLYy .

Please also check out a second-chance, workplace romance here, "**Heart of Stone Book 4**" https://books2read.com/u/4NXyPG with a host of characters intertwined.

What about dark romance that has everything from steamy romance, opposites attract, suspense, thriller, celebrity, and more "**Stolen:Fuertes Mafia Book 1**" https://books2read.com/u/mvZlgV

Catch up with favorite characters in this holiday short romance which includes spoilers. https://books2read.com/u/bzd59G

SNEAK PEEK

ANTONIO AND SABRINA STRUCK IN LOVE
BOOK 2

Sabrina

It's been a week already since my last meeting with my father to discuss the latest accounts. He's late, but then he usually is, so I take a second to check my phone for the hundredth time that morning. Antonio still hasn't called. Yeah, I'm crazy, and I should have just called him, but I know he's trouble. My heart couldn't take another breakup. I should forget about Antonio De Luca. My gut is telling me to do just that. He's probably looking for a one-night stand and I refuse to fall into another trap of loving a man again. At the same time, I tried to follow in Janice's footsteps and just be more carefree. *Who am I fooling?* I thought to myself. I couldn't just have a taste of Antonio De Luca and not fall for his sexy dominating ways. My heart was still fragile from Alex's cheating.

Finally, my father walked through the door. I stood up and gave him a kiss and a hug.

"How are you doing?" Dad asked.

"I'm great. How are you and Mom?"

"She wants you to call her to confirm dinner on Saturday with her and your sister Ashley ," my father answered.

"I'll call later when I'm off. What's Ashley doing back in town?"

"Who knows? I thought you'd have a clue, guess neither of us really pays attention to family dinners when in work mode." We laughed in agreement.

"Listen, Dad, I wanted to apologize for the other day in my office. I shouldn't have snapped at you. Alex was trying to get back with me by using you and Mom," I stated.

He waved me off.

"I'm sorry to. We shouldn't have gotten involved. You're a grown woman. You are perfectly capable of making your own decisions," he asserted, pinching my cheek and moving a strand of hair behind my ear.

I smiled at his endearing gesture.

"Thanks. So, let's get down to business, shall we?" I acknowledged.

"You want anything to eat? I can have Traci order in," Dad urged.

I nodded to go ahead and order as I looked over my desk to gather up my paperwork for our meeting. Pushing the thoughts of Antonio out of my head for the next few hours.

Antonio

Entering into the lobby of Washington Finance I stopped at the receptionist desk. We'd come here once before we knew Spencer's office was up on the twentieth floor but to avoid problems with security today, I followed protocol and let the receptionist do her job.

"I'm meeting with Spencer Jones. I'm Antonio De Luca," I stated, staring into the receptionist's eyes.

She stammered, "One moment… please."

After clearing her throat before speaking into the phone, "I have Antonio De Luca for Mr. Jones." Turning to me. "Yes, you're all set, Mr. De Luca. Head up to the twentieth floor, take the elevator and go to the right ." The receptionist pointed toward the doors of the elevator, and we headed up to the office. We stepped into the empty elevator and didn't speak as we took it to the twentieth floor. A loud ping told us we'd reached our destination.

"So, I need to tell you something," Carlo mentioned.

"What is it?" I asked.

I waited for Carlo to speak.

"When I was leaving the club the other day, heading to our meeting, I saw Bruno talking with Camilla. Then, last night, she popped back up at Ryde. I think they're up to something."

I could tell Carlo was getting angry. Whenever someone pissed him off, he'd start grinding his teeth. I needed to calm my irritation with the whole situation. I closed my eyes and pictured Sabrina under me, naked and moaning my name. If I found out Camilla and Bruno were working together in some way to hurt the Cartel or me, my father would have one less body to worry about.

"Let's get through this meeting, and we'll handle Bruno later."

"You're already dealing with your dad and brother; we need the Spain liquor deal to stick," Carlo stated.

"Yeah, we can't afford any distractions. I'll handle her. Let's get this going. I have plans later," I answered.

We entered Spencer's office. He shook our hands and motioned if we wanted a drink. Carlo and I waved off his offer and went to take a seat in front of his desk.

"So, gentlemen, I understand you own multiple clubs

and other businesses, and you've just signed a deal with Spaniard Liqueur and Wine for ten million dollars?" Spencer asked, as he pulled up the information on his computer.

"Yes, that's correct, and I wanted to get six million of that invested, and two percent distributed back into the clubs for more development and promotion."

Hopefully, he'd be able to work this through his company. The last thing I needed was the Feds looking at my books.

"Sounds like a plan. Can I see the contract so we can begin the process? Just so we have a clear understanding, the standard fee at Washington Finance is one point five million for all opening investments. Is that a problem?" Spencer questioned. Spencer narrowed his eyes at me, then Carlo, who had a smirk on his face. He thought we couldn't pull this off.

Carlo opened up the bag that held two points and one million in cash, and he handed it off to Spencer as I sat back with a wide grin.

"That won't be a problem, I can assure you," I said smugly.

Carlo poured everything out of the bag.

An hour after signing the paperwork, Carlo and I walked out of Spencer's office and headed toward the elevators when suddenly we bumped into a woman who looked all too familiar. All of her papers landed on the ground. We bent down to help her gather her work from the floor. Snapping my fingers when it came to me, I recalled that she was Sabrina's friend, Janice.

"I'm so sorry. I didn't see you coming," Janice muttered.

Janice grabbed the papers out of my hands.

"No problem," Carlo replied.

Carlo lingered onto the papers he was holding, trying to hold onto Janice's hand.

They both spoke at the same time.

"I know you," I mumbled.

"You have got to be shitting me!" she shouted.

"Excuse me?" I challenged.

READING ORDER OF STRUCK IN LOVE UNIVERSE

Order of Reading

The Early Years-A Prequel Short Story
https://books2read.com/u/49Zjnw
Ruthless Struck In Love Book 1
https://books2read.com/u/4AxKLo
Savage Struck In Love Book 2
https://books2read.com/u/bpED6g
Beast Struck In Love Book 3
https://books2read.com/u/3LpgdJ
Janice and Carlo Captivated By His Love
https://books2read.com/u/b6je6M
Brutal Struck In Love Book 4
https://books2read.com/u/4NQyE9
Joaquin Fuertes-The Fuertes Cartel Book 1
https://books2read.com/u/mvZlgV
Joaquin Fuertes-The Fuertes Cartel Book 2
https://books2read.com/u/4DWwLd
Redemption Struck In Love Book 5
https://books2read.com/u/b5kZ8O

Joaquin Fuertes-The Fuertes Cartel Book 3
https://books2read.com/u/4A5LGp

READING ORDER HEART OF STONE

Heart of Stone Book 1 Emery and Jackson
  https://books2read.com/u/boWPAV
  Heart of Stone Book 1.5
  https://books2read.com/u/mKELYZ
  Heart of Stone Book 2 Jordan and Damon
  https://books2read.com/u/ba2OMx
  Heart of Stone Book 3.5 Bottoms Up
  https://books2read.com/u/4EkjBg
  Heart of Stone Book 3 Angela and Brent
  https://books2read.com/u/31rx9l
  Heart of Stone Book 4 Jessica and Joseph
  https://books2read.com/u/4NXyPG

WHAT'S NEXT

Want to know what happens next?

Follow me on my website to catch the next release.

Reviews are the lifeblood of the publishing world. They're read, appreciated, and needed.

Please consider taking the time to leave a few words on your review platform of choice.

Sign up for updates and sneak peaks at the site below.
www.chiquitadennie.com

CATALOG RELEASES

The Early Years-A Prequel Short Story
Antonio and Sabrina: Struck in Love 1, 2, 3,4,5
Heart of Stone, Book 1 (Emery & Jackson)
Heart Of Stone Book 1.5 Emery &Jackson A Valentine's Day Short
Janice and Carlo: Captivated By His Love
Heart of Stone, Book 2 (Jordan and Damon)
Temptation
Heart of Stone, Book 3 (Angela and Brent)
Bottoms Up Heart of Stone, Book 3.5(Jessica and Joseph Short
Cocky Catcher
Bossy Billionaire
Love Shorts:A Collection of Short Stories
Joaquin Fuertes (The Fuertes Cartel Book 1)
Exposed (Salvation Society Novel)
Joaquin Fuertes (The Fuertes Cartel Book 2)
Refuel(A Driven World Novel)
Pressure(A Driven World Novel)

Until Serena(HEA World Novel)
Exposed (Salvation Society Novel)
Heart of Stone, Book 4 (Jessica and Joseph)
She's All I Need
Something Gaine(Romantic Comedy)

PLAYLIST

1.Beyonce: 7/11
   2.Rihanna: Cockiness
   3.Heather Headley: In My Mind
   4.Imagine Dragons: Radioactive
   5.Tank: When We
   6.Jazmine Sullivan: Insecure
   7.Rick James & Teena Marie: Fire and Desire
   8.The Temptations: Ain't Too Proud To Beg
   9.The Supremes: You Keep Hanging On
   10.Rihanna: Love On The Brain

304 PUBLISHING COMPANY

The home of authors African American, Interracial, Women's Fiction, Fantasy, Erotic, and Contemporary Romance novels. Along with Thriller, Suspense, Poetry, Beauty, and Style Books. Thank you for taking the time out to visit. Join our mailing list to stay updated with new releases and blog posts.

ACKNOWLEDGMENTS

I want to dedicate this to my team that helps me behind the scenes, from my editors, test readers, graphic designers, and the list goes on. Truly appreciate each of you for keeping me on my toes.

ABOUT THE AUTHOR

Chiquita Dennie is an emerging author of romance. This is her seventeenth book, and Award winning Filmmaker. Her first short film "Invisible" released in Summer 2017 and screened in multiple festivals and won for Best Short Film. Also, she hosts a podcast that showcases the latest in Beauty, Business, and Community called "Moscato and Tea." Her debut release of Antonio and Sabrina: Struck In Love has opened a new avenue of writing that she loves.

Chiquita lives in Los Angeles, CA. Before she started writing contemporary romance, worked in the entertainment industry on notable TV shows such as: Dr Phil show, Tyra Banks show, American Idol, and Deal or No Deal. But her favorite job is the one she's no doing full time, writing romance.

If you want to know when the next book will come out, please visit my website at www.chiquitadennie.com, where you can sign up to receive an email for my next release.